DEVELOPMENTAL

EMILY FOX-DOUGLAS

Contents

*A mother understands
what a child does not say.*

—Jewish proverb

Prologue

In the weeks after Rudy was born, I lay awake, drenched in postpartum sweat, hearing the howling of wolves in my ears. Night after night, they circle closer to the broken, white pickets surrounding our chipped-paint lavender cottage. The sounds of their teeth snapping outside the window leave me gasping and running to his bassinet. I nurse him most nights, clutching his body to my breast in tight-fisted desperation, staring at the shadowed backyard.

I didn't tell Riya immediately about the dark, canine shadows that call out to me from just beyond the yard. They stay close to the fence line, skulking and amorphous. It is easy to write them off as a trick of the eye—sleep deprivation demons of the newly minted mother—until the streetlights catch the metal glint in their eyes. A flash of silver iris, like a lighthouse bulb spinning before blinking out into the dark, churning sea.

I think about my mother and the days before she left us at my grandmother's house and didn't come back for a very long time. I think about the way she pulled the drywall off in neat chunks, meticulously checking each piece as if she were a jeweler spying for imperfections, turning each section with careful precision before placing it in a crumpled Revco shopping bag.

"This is where they put the bugs," she would tell us when we asked her what she was doing. "That's how they can hear you, everything you say, everything you do." Her eyes shone with the glittering emerald of what I now know was madness. She grabbed my shoulder and pulled me close, her metallic breath burning my face, tinged with Merit Ultra-Lights and Midwest methamphetamine. "I will never let them come for us, baby".

Thinking she was talking about real bugs, I nodded my head in agreement. I hated the bugs in our apartment and the way they would run for the corners when you flipped on the lights. I hated how they made my little sister cry in the dark when they ran across her face while she tried to sleep, their legs like dirty eyelashes stuck to her skin.

My mother's eyes were fire those nights, watching the corners for things we could not see. I wonder if she were here, could she see the wolves too, running suicides back and forth just beyond the fence? I watch the walls of Rudy's nursery, willing myself not to pick at the cracks in the plaster.

Riya offers to stay up with the baby, but I won't let her. I am determined to be all the things my mother wasn't—all the things my sister would never get to be. In our marriage, I am the one prone to emotional peaks and valleys, while she tends toward dogged practicality. A chemical engineer who had risen quickly in her career due to her precise and pragmatic mind, Riya is my true north when the compass went spinning and Rudy had spun the compass. No one can truly prepare you for how much parenthood changes the direction of your life, but Riya believed in me. She believed me in a way that only people who have never watched their mother pick the walls apart can believe in you. However, I know what happens to mothers who see things that no one else can see. They go far away, and they never come back.

These days, the wolves and I keep our own company.

7 Months

Rudy has a special way of entertaining himself with his hands. The doctor says that all babies do it, but when Rudy watches his hands, it's like he is watching a meteor shower—amazed by the constellations his fingers make in the sky. It is one of the few times he seems content. Deep in bouts of colic, he strains and stretches his tiny body in a battle onto himself. No amount of rocking, swaddling, or swaying causes him to raise the white flag. We sleep for blackened, two-hour stints only to wake, fists raised for another round of combat.

The sky is dusky, and he looks up from his silent symphony while we are looking out the back window. Rudy giggles and flaps his arms. He looks beyond me into the dawn breaking over the backyard. I attempt to razz his belly. He glances at the space beside me before returning his attention to the window.

"What do you see, little bear?" I ask, following his gaze in bemused exhaustion. It has been weeks since I have seen the wolves, and I had almost forgotten them—almost, but not quite.

The air behind the fence shimmers in an otherworldly way that first seems like a trick of the eye, but then the disorganized air takes shape. It is a man standing at the fence in dark blue coveralls. I raise my hand tentatively to wave, thinking he could be a neighbor, but he doesn't look familiar. I lean closer, squinting. He is tall, at least six-foot-five, maybe more. The pickets of the fence, which reach my ribs when I lean over it, do not even clear his thighs, which bulge under the coveralls. Resting one hand on the fence, he appears to be clutching a fist full of weeds.

I step closer, nose almost touching the glass.

Focusing my tired eyes on the plants, I realize he is not holding uprooted plants—the plants are part of his hands. The joints are white like upended garlic bulbs and fibrous root hairs cover the knuckles. He pulls his right arm from behind his back and rests it next to his left hand on the fence.

The skin on his forearms appears rotten and stretched, breaking through in places to show sinews of muscle underneath. Running through the slabs of muscle are ghost white root systems that disappear under the rolled-up arms of the coveralls.

He looks at me with a curious and intent gaze. I feel suddenly exhausted and my head droops, first gradually, then snapping down and up in the way of the very, very tired. Rudy lies still in my arms, staring back at the man with a smile. *Don't drop the baby, a voice from far inside me warns.*

The man raises one arm, slowly, and crooks a soil-covered finger out in front of him, pulling it back fluidly one, two, three times, beckoning us to the fence. Rudy giggles in delight. Feeling hazy and dreamlike, I step forward. The air smells hypnotic around me, like chamomile and cannabis and lavender and freshly baked bread, all rolled into one intoxicating scent. I breathe in deeply and close my eyes.

The man smiles and I can see flecks of green plant matter are matted to his neck and arms. Tiny thorns protrude from his beard and thick arm hair. Under the beard, he pulls back his lips and reveals a yellow-white set of canine teeth, pointed and glistening with saliva.

I step back, alarm flooding my drugged senses and his placid face transforms into menace, as if metabolizing my fear. A low growl escapes through his bared teeth. The air around him shimmers and he is gone.

Rudy is inconsolable for the rest of the day. The screams morph into one horrendous sound, overtaking all other sounds. I feel like I am standing in the tunnel of the scream, and all else had ceased to exist. I had ceased to exist. Now I know why the nurses in Labor and Delivery had been so adamant that we watch the films on Shaken Baby Syndrome before we would be allowed discharge.

My hands turn floaty, and I wonder would they move of their own accord. Time melted and felt both limitless and like every second was an hour. I place Rudy in his crib and turn, walking from the room like I had left my body. Over his screams, I switch the fan on high and jam earplugs in place. When the darkness came, I wish it would dig deep, burying me into a bottomless hole where no light would ever reach me again.

I awake to Riya shaking me. The air smells acrid, and the light looks long and shadowed. I have slept through the day.

"Eloise, you left a candle burning, and the house was filled with smoke when I got home. You're lucky you didn't burn the fucking house down!" she yells.

"I-I—" I try to find the words as I wipe the sleep out of my eyes. Did I light a candle? I don't remember.

I am suddenly enraged, remembering the three times I had been up that night, to try to give her a full night of sleep before she pitched a big project to the department heads this afternoon. All while she is begrudging me a simple nap. I sit up in bed and toss the Afghan aside.

"Three hours Riya. He screamed for three goddamn hours. I needed sleep. I needed…something."

Riya takes a deep breath and closes her eyes. "How did you not hear the smoke alarm?" she says, measured.

I shake my head and shrug, shoving the earplugs deep into the pocket of my sweatpants. It's best she doesn't know that some days the earplugs were all that kept Rudy and I from going the wrong way off the crying bridge.

"What can I do? Do you need help? We can hire a nanny?" she asks, softening. She adds quietly, "I think you should talk to Dr. Kim."

Her face is worried. I am another problem that needed fixing. A nanny for what, I think. I don't *do* anything. I stay in this house all day and *don't do anything*. I can't even comfort my child—my literal only job at the moment.

I am disappearing. Soon I will vanish, like the man at the fence. I will go wherever it is that wolves go.

14 Months

G o," Rudy demands, his fists opening and closing as he stood in front of the TV—two feet of concrete toddler insistence that I am no match for.

I sigh and push the laptop aside, knowing there is no waiting with Rudy. *Demands must be met immediately* was circled on the paperwork for the developmental pediatrician with whom we were meeting later in the month. Demands must be met immediately, indeed.

"Go! Go!" he says again, his tone rising in urgency.

I mash the buttons on the remote, trying to get the movie

to restart. It stays frozen midway through the opening sequence of 101 Dalmatians. Pongo is mid-stride, one leg poised in the air, on his way to follow the beautiful lady dog, blissfully unaware of the adventure that lies ahead.

"Maummaum. Go. Go. Go." He stamps his foot in frustration and places my hand on the TV.

I can feel the meltdown coming. Not meeting the Dalmatian demand immediately would result not in a typical toddler tantrum that you could wait out. No, it would result in a five-alarm fire meltdown that raised concern from the neighbors that Rudy was being thrown into walls or having his bones broken, when the truth was I had failed to get the movie to start quickly enough.

I restart the router as he screams. The pain that had threatened to erupt behind my temples all day blooms into a full-blown tension headache. I check my phone. Sure enough, our neighborhood is under an internet outage. All the work from home neighbors are having their own meltdown in the neighborhood social media group.

I groan. We are in for a long afternoon.

He cries and grabs my hands, placing them over and over again on the TV.

"It's broken baby bear, broken. See, won't work". I motion to the TV sitting black and imposing in the living room.

"Go, go, go," he implores, tears streaming down his

cheeks.

I rock him while he bangs his head into my chest, every muscle in his body tensed into a tight knot. My teeth are clenched so tightly I fear they will crack. I see his smeared handprints on the TV where he has pushed the screen again and again. It faces the front window, reflecting back at us the silhouette of the lilac bush that sways in the breeze. I watch the screen as the bush shakes and a rustling sound comes from the front porch through the open window.

I cringe inwardly, thinking about how the neighbors could hear every scream from Rudy and prayed that they wouldn't call the cops or, worse, talk shit about me on the neighborhood block watch page. Not with my name, of course, but some comment like; *Need advice hive mind. Neighbor has a little boy who won't stop screaming. I know toddlers cry, but I am worried something more is going on because he screams for hours. Should I call the police? Go over and offer to help?*.

The rustling in the bushes continues. In between Rudy's cries, I hear a low growl. The rustling erupts into a full-on thrashing. The lilac bush shakes furiously, and a shrill, desperate yelp calls out, followed by a sound like branches snapping and deafening growl. The house vibrates into the floorboards under my bare feet. I dash to the front door and snap the lock, imagining some slick-coated predator crashing through the screen and snatching up Rudy in his teeth.

The ruckus has silenced Rudy's cries, and he looks at the front door in curiosity, the movie finally forgotten. Whatever was in the yard seems to be gone. The birds have resumed their midday song. A jogger runs by, headphones in and oblivious to anything out of the ordinary.

I look out the window, still unsettled by the feral animal sounds from just moments before. I pull back the curtain and hiss a sharp intake of breath. Sitting on the porch, center to the window, is a large rabbit. Fresh blood swirls around the porch slats, still wet from the kill. I feel a cry rising in my throat and try to swallow it down. Two small shapes orbit the rabbit, pushing their tiny heads into the unmoving torso—orphans from the kill. The babies are crawling up their mother's body, willing her to move and continue to be their lighthouse against harsh seas.

At that moment, the TV springs back to life and the opening credits to 101 Dalmatians start. Rudy squeals and flaps his arms, waving them up and down in a happy toddler dance. He chants my name like a mantra, "Maum, Maum, Maum."

I close the door.

21 Months

In the summer we take refuge in the deep double-lot of the backyard. The previous owners cultivated blueberries, which had run riot over wired arches and pressed against overgrown flower beds I had neither interest nor time for. An old cobblestone patio surrounded the back of the home. The entire rear portion of the property is ensconced in a rather useless white picket fence. When we had bought the house, Riya and I joked that we were buying the American dream, complete with a white picket fence.

The back part of the fence is more honeysuckle than

fence. A towering bush stands otherworldly in between our home and the elementary school. The unused original schoolhouse is just across the fence. The realtor had warned them they would be renovating the building back to its former glory just as soon as the next bond passed. Years came and went, and the brick building remained handsomely empty and ivy strewn.

Recently, Rudy had begun to sleep through the night and with it his disposition lifted dramatically. It is time both precious and fleeting. We spend our days lolling on my grandmother's old quilt, under the branches of an elm. The summer has turned into a warm reprieve after the hurricane that was Rudy's first year. He sits contentedly with me, arranging a collection of small animal figurines into marching band ready lines on the blanket. I lose myself in the pages of Virginia Woolf, stopping only to reapply sunblock and adjust Rudy's sunhat. All around us hums a chorus of insects and chirping birds.

I look down and see the bottom of the coffee cup. Riya and I had stayed up late, watching movies and making love. It had been a good night and well worth the sleep we had both missed. My mouth waters at the memory and craves another cup of coffee.

Rudy does not look up from his toys when I stand.

"Rudy," I say.

He continues to play.

"Rudy," I say, this time a little louder.

He ignores me and I try once more before giving up and walking into the house. It is like he lives in a world wholly different from mine. He is there, alongside me in everything we do, but existing on some kind of parallel plane—his body there, but his mind somewhere in the atmosphere. Still, he is my world, and I am determined to be the planet he orbits.

When I return with a fresh cup of coffee, Rudy is gone.

This is odd, as he rarely leaves the blanket, disliking the feeling of grass on his bare feet and preferring to spend his time arranging dog figurines in quiet contentment. He will only occasionally wander if something interesting enough catches his attention, like a garden pinwheel or the sound of an approaching garbage truck.

Anxiety rises in my chest as I scan the backyard.

"Rudy!" I yell.

I hear only the birds chirping and the far-off sound of a radio playing big-band music. I set the cup down and call his name again, more urgently this time, looking around the backyard.

After twenty minutes of searching, hysteria is closing in. I run back into the house to get my phone and call Riya. I look down at her name on my contact list, hesitating. Ever since the day of the smoke alarms and the man at the fence, I am leary of telling her anything that might alarm her further. With shaking hands, I begin to type a text asking her to come home at once when a strange buzzing sound covers the backyard.

It takes me a moment to locate the sound, which is coming from the enormous honeysuckle bush at the back of the yard. As I walk closer, I see a swarm of bees covering the bush in an arch. They appear to be converging on the outer edges of the plant. Their buzzing is like an orchestra of the surreal calling her name.

He's here.

The thought comes unbidden in my head and is directly followed by an image of Rudy disappearing into the honeysuckle like a fox darting into the underbrush. I look again at the plant. It's twisted into a crooked arch, the blooms surrounding a darkened space like a wreath. I run the rest of the way to the fence and drop to my knees before the void, the sickly-sweet smell of the tiny white flowers turning my stomach.

Through the branches and vine, I see a dark space pierced through shards of light. I push my head through the opening and gasp. The rot in the wood has given way to a space no bigger than fourteen inches across—just the right size for a small animal or tiny human to push through.

I rear back, and kick the edges of the rotted fence away, widening the hole. With desperation, I haul my body through, not even flinching as a splinter of wood rips through my thin linen pants, tearing the skin beneath. The wood cracks and gives way with a snap as I tumble out through the other side of the fence.

"Rudy!" I scream.

I look around the vacant lot. The closed schoolhouse rises out of the weeds like an ancient ruin. It is an older style building of three stories. A decrepit black metal exterior staircase marches up the back of the building. Every inch of the property mocks me with the places it could hide my baby. Every direction I look, I face another sharp edge that could kill him; the back cement lot covered in nails, the loosely boarded windows hung haphazardly, waiting for a small nudge to send them flying down the ground below, bits of broken glass. But the stairs are by far the worst.

They rise up three stories of black, rusted steel. Holes the size of a fist shine through with sharp ridges of sunlight. It appears to almost sway in the wind. I know before I even set one foot on it that it will buck under my weight. Rudy would be drawn to it, loving to climb any set of stairs he could find; delighting in the heights he could now mount all by himself.

I step up the first step and scream his name and my blood turns to ice. Instead of hearing Rudy, the sound of children's laughter drifts down the fire escape from the floors above.

There are no children here.

This has not been an operational school for thirty years. I know this, yet the laughter sounds again, louder this time. I look wildly around the area, frantically trying to locate the source. The next time I hear the laughter, it is right behind me. I whip my head around and see nothing besides cracked concrete and weeds. I feel something wet on my side and when I look down, I see blood soaking through the hip of my pants where I had ripped my skin on the broken fence. My head swims with dizziness.

"R-Ru-Rudy!"

Struggling to catch my breath, I listen for him, praying the phantom children would stay quiet enough for me to find him. I hear a creak above my head. My heart leaps into my throat as I hear a familiar sound.

"Maum-Maum-Maum-Maum-Maum."

Rudy's babble. I would know it anywhere, as familiar as my pulse. A scuffling sound was coming from the steps above. Rudy was moving! I sprint up the stairs, willing myself to ignore how far apart the metal bars were set; how easily a toddler could squeeze through those gaping spaces.

On the third-floor landing, Rudy sits with his back facing a pitch-black open doorway. The door hangs open into the midnight interior of the school. He smiles and begins pumping his arms when he sees me. I close the distance between us and snatch him up with a speed I didn't know possible.

Clutching him to my breast, I turn around and begin to descend the swaying staircase.

I feel him before I see him. The man from the fence.

He stands in the doorway, more shadow than person. Too tall, he steps from the doorway of the long-abandoned classroom into the sunlight. I stand frozen, one foot on the stair behind me, poised to run. He wears an old-fashioned suit this time, but his skin looks awful where it peeks out at the hands and neck. It is rough, textured, and covered in small thorns and thistle. He is sallow; the color of earthworms and grubs. He is alleyways and construction lots and fauna peeking through the garbage. He smells of unwanted living things, fed with urine and spilled oil cans, vicious brambles pushing through broken concrete to chase out sunlight.

"Man-man," Rudy babbles, then goes silent, staring into the man's awful eyes.

A blast of radio static burst through the air. Somewhere in the distance, a neighbor turns up their radio and I hear the familiar strains of an old song, one my grandfather used to play. *Stickers*, he would say. *Honey, you got stuck with a sticker*. The man's skin looks like sticker weeds, the thorny sharp weeds you see in overgrown fields and abandoned lots across the Midwest.

The Stickerman's face clouds with anger as he looks in the direction of the music. As his attention shifts, I take another step down.

He licks his lips and a gray, forked tongue flits out from his cracked lips. He looks at us hungrily and steps forward, his eyes locked on my waist—on Rudy. I stumble back, grab the rusted handrail, and sprint down the stairs. A burning pain shoots through my shoulder as the man clamps his massive hand on me. Tears and pain cloud my eyes and I wrench forward, clearing the second story in what feels like seconds.

I hear wood splintering and feel the stairs sway under our weight. Paint chips and grit rain down from his thundering footsteps above us. A burst of adrenaline thrusts my legs forward in one final push. I clear the stairs and take off for the fence. In one motion, I toss Rudy through the hole in the honeysuckle as he cries quietly.

Back in our yard, I glance back and, to my surprise, see the lot and stairs are empty. The third-floor door that was hanging open only moments before, is closed and boarded up. In shock, I run to the garage and pull out an old wooden door we had stashed in the back, hoping to refinish and hang back in the house. Holding it up with my bleeding hip, I hammer it over the hole in the fence with one hand while holding Rudy by my other. I think about the baby bunnies, covered in their mother's blood.

24 Months

No, no, no, no. A swelling of anxiety washes over me as Rudy stirs in his bed. I fight back tears as I look at the clock: 2:17 a.m. I can't do another three months of sleep deprivation. Some animal scratching at the back door had already woken me three of the past seven nights. Now Rudy is waking up every night again. I wait for his cry, one foot on the woven carpet, one foot on the bed.

I sit up, listening. Riya rolls over and opens her eyes.

"He's fine," she says, reaching over to wrap one arm around my neck, pulling me back to bed.

I fight the urge to check the fence. I had already checked it twice after dinner, wiggling the slats to check for weakness in the structure, eyeing the perimeter for holes. Riya had been astounded when I had cleaned out half our savings account to pay for the new eight-foot privacy fence.

"We need it for security," I insisted, and Riya had relented. She understands my need for safety at all costs.

"Maum, Maum, Maum. Hi, Maum."

I feel my body relax as I heard him hum my name and recall the fitness of each fence plank.

***

Night hangs over my bedroom like spilled ink. My eyes fight the indigo shadows and struggle to find purchase on anything solid. Shapes shift in and out of view while the layers of sleep lift. Unsure of what has wakened me, I turn on my side and wait, listening for my son.

The radiator kicks on just as Rudy begins to vocalize and I relax. Those are happy sounds.

"Go. Hi go!" he says.

Something in the engagement of his voice gives me pause. There is a slight change in tone. This is the voice he uses when he talks to someone else. This is his seldom heard conversational voice. Unconsciously, I reach for Riya and remember she is away for work. A spike of adrenaline shoots through my body.

Someone is in the house. Someone not us.

I creep from my bedroom into the hallway and stand outside his door and listen.

"Hi, go, hi!" Rudy giggles.

The house sighs around me and whispers from the bedroom draw me closer. I look inside and the sky-blue walls are a wash of faded gray. The glow of a night-light shoots stars up the far wall all the way to the ceiling. My skin prickles with electricity like the moment before a storm.

Rudy stands facing the wall with his back to me. His little arms wave up and down excitedly, clearly enchanted by whatever or whoever is before him.

"Go, hi, go go go go."

I watch in astonishment as a shadow peels itself off the wall. It is the shape of a dog, but somehow different. Its legs pulled out like malformed taffy; the dog extends into the dark corners of the wall in exaggerated menace. Its head twists back, a silhouette of a jaw snapping. I can hear his jaw click.

The wolves had made it inside.

"Go, hi go! Go, hi Go!" Rudy exclaims, rocking his body while energetically flapping his arms.

The shadow moves towards Rudy's crib, and I shoot through the door, slamming the light on. Rudy screams. In my arms, he writhes and looks towards the window facing the backyard.

"Go, go. Ack ack go?"

"Shh, baby. Shhh. It's ok. There's no one there."

"Go, go. Ack ack go?" over and over he asks.

As I am stroking his chubby arm, my fingers graze over a series of bumps. Still bouncing him in my arms, I move closer to the lamp and switch it on. I suck in a sharp inhale of breath through my teeth and grimace. Small scratches and pockmarks of raised skin cover his whole left arm. The worst run up his forearm in an angry spiral like a nocturnal octopus had hooked him with its tentacles to pull him down into a dreamsea. Rudy does not seem to notice and instead is fixating on the wall where the dog shadow had been.

"Go?" he asks, looking at the space behind me.

"All gone, puppy gone," I say.

"Uppy gone uppy gone upp gone. Bye go. Go. Go." He resumes humming and bouncing back and forth in my arms.

I sit on the floor of his room long after he has fallen back asleep and wait for my heartbeat to stop racing. I wonder how long it will be before I too will pick the plaster off his walls, looking for what lies beneath. An image runs on a loop in my mind. In the dog's hasty retreat, a thin line of light had shone from around his neck as if it was held taut by some unseen hand.

Rudy's longdog was on a leash, held by a hand of thorns.

28 Months

Riya's looks linger on me these days, and I pretend they don't. I no longer hide my nightly fence checks. At dusk, I walk the perimeter of the backyard, running my fingers across the fence, testing its sturdiness, and looking for gaps and imperfections. I feel the old schoolhouse looming behind the fence like some sort of leviathan. In the small snatches of sleep I steal, I see tiny fist-sized holes in the fence that I look through and see the bricks of the school. I hear the laughter of children and see thorny leaves pushing through the spaces, making a way to bring

Rudy back to them—back to him.

The marks reappear on Rudy. Sometimes they will be on his foot. Other times, bumps rise up across his side.

"It's just eczema," Riya says. "Did you try the honey balm my sister gave us?"

I don't know how to tell her about what is coming. I am afraid she will keep him from me if I tell her why I'm scared; what I have seen. I'm afraid to admit to myself what I've seen. I feel him. The shadow man with an embrace of thorns who calls to my son like a Pied Piper.

I snatch the canister of balm from her hands, silent and irrationally angry. It is so easy for her, sleeping uninterrupted in hotel rooms for days, even weeks, at a time. When she returns home, she just machetes her way through the underbrush that is our world, clueless and destructive, clearing a path for Him.

"I'm just worried about you," Riya whispers to my back in bed.

"I'm fine," I lie.

I wake to Rudy's voice.

"Ella, eh, ville, ella, eh, ville," he chants.

That is a new word I hadn't heard him say before. The house sighs and just under the sound of the air conditioner, I hear a faint scratching, like a hand running across the window in a whisper. It sounds just enough out of place to slither unease through my guts.

ella ehville ella ehville ella eville

***

August drops onto Arcadia like a picnic blanket soaked from the rain; heavy, hot, and wet. The morning's quiet is accompanied by the dull hum of the air conditioner pulling its weight against the already deepening heat of the day. Rudy dumps a container of animal figurines on the carpet and sorts them into circles by breed. A small ring of terriers rests next to the larger ring of many-sized dalmatians. He kisses the noses of all the dogs and sets them down until together they make one concentric canine snowflake. Rudy brings his pudgy cheeks to the floor and examines his creation with a practiced eye. Satisfied, he sits up, squeals, and waves two hands into the air in front of him.

I blow steam off my second cup of coffee when a sound catches my attention. Rather, the absence of sound catches my attention. The house is quiet in a way that it usually was not at this time of the day. I checked the lights—working. The electricity was on. *Shit, the a/c.*

The air conditioner is silent. My armpits are dampening with sweat and Rudy's cheeks are pinker than usual. The room is stuffy and warm. I jam my fingers desperately into the buttons of the thermostat—nothing. Glancing back at Rudy and finding him still immersed in dog toys, I make my way to the backyard.

The air conditioner unit sits hulking and silent in the bright late morning sun. Weeds grow up all around it, but nothing seems to be jamming the fan apparatus. A chill runs down my back. Out of nowhere, my son's song from the last seven nights ran through my head.

Ellaehvilleellaehville.

Rudy fights sleep that night, and both our moods are sour from the immersive heat. He's cranky and butts his head against my chest over and over like a small animal burrowing for comfort.

"Go. go?" Rudy says.

"Okay, let's find Go," I reply.

We walk around the house until I spy the Pongo figurine peeking out from under the coffee table. Rudy clutches the dog in his sweaty toddler fists and gurgles happy noises. Finally, at one in the morning, his eyes begin to droop, and he lets me put him in bed.

I feel uneasy as I didn't have a chance to check the fence that evening. The thought of going into the backyard alone, leaving Rudy unattended, fills me with familiar apprehension. Instead, I double and triple-check the locks on the door, worrying as I flip the deadbolts that he will wander from his room, and I will lose him to the songs of the honeysuckle.

Despite the heat, the cricket song from the open windows lure me into a restless sleep. When Rudy's laughter wakes me several hours later, the clock next to my bed is blank, and the room is silent. I flip the lamp switch and nothing happens. The power is out.

I follow his sounds and call his name, stopping in front of his empty bed.

"Go! Hi Go!" Rudy's baby voice drifts from another room.

I look around frantically to locate the sound, my eyes landing on the open window, curtains wafting in the breeze. The screen is pushed up, gaping silently at the darkened backyard. I can just make out his shape in the back corner. He isn't alone. Rudy runs in circles and behind him was a dog, or the approximation of a dog, nipping at his heels while he laughs in delight.

"Rudy, stay right there. I'm coming," I yell.

He doesn't turn and keeps running with the dog, circle after circle. The dog, whose shadow looks more shadow than solid shape. The dog who seemed stretched a little longer than a regular dog, like someone had made a German Shepherd from clay, then pulled at its tail and nose until he yelped, and then abandoned the stretched monstrosity.

I push the window screen up and tumble into the back garden. By the time I stand, they are gone. There is no sign of Rudy and his too-long dog. I hear a child's laugh coming from the very end of the backyard, from the honeysuckle.

I know what I will find at the back fence before I see it.

A perfect hobbit-hole in the blooming honeysuckle. The two main branches cross over itself, making a fairy gate right to the back of the closed school. I peel back the leaves and look through the wreath to see two small feet running past the fence.

Reaching for him, my fingers graze his heels and just miss latching onto his pajamaed leg. I tumble after him with a cry.

"Ma, ma!" he says, arms flapping. He points to the inky dog running up the school stairs. "Go!" he says excitedly and takes off after the dog.

Tears stream down my face as I run after him. I know I need to stop and call for help. Still screaming his name, I press the numbers 9-1-1, but before I can hit send, a blistering pain rips through my arm and I drop the phone.

"No!" I scream.

A deep growl vibrates the ground and from the weeds rises a man, dark and terrible. His legs are thick and ropey as roots, carrying him to at least seven feet in height. His arms bulge, skin splitting to show vine, thorn, and nettle underneath. A thick residue coats his entire body like a viscous sap.

He lets out a sharp whistle and the long dog returns to his side. Up close, the dog is not happy and friendly. It is boney and starved, ribs poking out from its gray fur. Black spots that were apparent when he was next to Rudy, fade and fall like ash from his fur when he returns to his master.

Rudy does not notice and has changed course to run after the dog; hands opening and closing in front of him like a joy-seeking radar.

"Go," he cries. "Go! Go!"

"Rudy, no!" I scream.

I pull myself up after him. The Stickerman slams my body to the ground and howls in laughter.

Rudy stares at the man and begins to furiously speak. "Ella! Ma, it Ella. It Ella De Ville," he cries.

It finally clicks. Ella, Cruella Deville. The Cruel Devil. Rudy's only idea of a villain. I make another grab for my phone, but longdog's teeth clamp down on my wrist so hard I hear the bones pop. When the pain does come through, it is long, and deep, and sharp.

Longdog's legs are on my chest. I struggle to breathe—he is stronger than he looks. He holds me down and I see Stickerman coming closer. His arms don't reach as much as they grow—extending vines on spiky tendrils that wrap around the body like ropes. The smaller stickers scratch my skin, and the larger thorns break it open. I sob as he drags me away from Rudy, who is crying alone in the weeds. Something akin to drowsiness creeps over me. His vines are full of a poison that pulls me under. I look at Rudy one last time and keep my directions simple.

"Rudy, baby. Run!"

35 Months, One Week

The first light of dawn is breaking over the east. The horizon over the schoolhouse lights up pink and brown in a tie-dyed tapestry of factory emissions and ozone. It has been one week since his third birthday, and I am completely unmoored. I look at him and know he is changed. We both are.

Riya returned home from the airport to find me unconscious on the chaise lounge in the backyard. The blood on my shoulder had caked and dried to my pajamas in a stiff coating. When she shook me awake, I tried to run back to the schoolhouse, sputtering disconnected words about finding Rudy. She assured me he was sleeping peacefully in his room and caught me before I fell onto the cobblestones.

For almost a week, I slept and lived in the in-between spaces of awake and unconsciousness. I dreamed of my mother pulling the plaster from the walls of my room, revealing staggeringly thick root systems that pulsated like veins and boomed a rhythm of heartbeats in my dream. From them burst tiny white leaves the color of maggots, covered in minuscule thorns that dripped venomous red sap. I was pulled into nightmares that opened up into new ones like a never-ending set of Russian nesting dolls.

When I came to, Rudy spoke to me, and anyone else who would listen, for that matter. Almost overnight, he began speaking fully and in complete sentences. I knew I should feel grateful, but I couldn't shake the suspicion that he just wasn't *him* anymore. I tried to hide the paranoia (plaster chunks in a Revco bag), but Riya saw through me.

"It's like you want something to be wrong with him, Eloise. It's weird. It just took him longer to start talking. He's fine." She drew out the last word with annoyed emphasis.

"I know, I just…" *Miss him.* I struggle to say the last two words out loud.

He sits in the middle of a scattered pile of birthday toys. Smiling, he brings his new Paw Patrol toy to show Riya. I hold my arms out for a hug and he ducks, returning to the mess of plastic on the floor. The new set of Safari Limited dogs lies untouched under a table.

"No, Mama Elle, I playing paw troll now," he says.

I give him a tight smile and hide my tears. I know I should be happy. He was playing with his toys and not spending hours arranging them without looking up to notice the world around him. But the Mama Elle killed me. I hear his baby voice calling from the past. It is my heartbeat. *Maum, Maum, Maum.*

When those same words wake me later that night, I smile in the dark.

"Maummaummaum…"

Rudy's voice carries faintly through the vents. His old voice. The hardwood floor seeps cold through my thick socks as I pad into the hall to check on him.

His room is dark except for the night-light. He sleeps soundly in his bed, his tiny hands drawn up to his neck. He reminds me of my baby—my sweet, singing baby who loves sounds more than words. Who is both distant and inexorably attached to me by the golden soul-cord. He is the island and the sea between.

"Hi, Maummaummaum. See Go?"

The voice comes from far away, but not from the tiny body asleep in the bed. I resist the urge to place my ear against the plaster. There is nothing in the walls. *There is no one in the walls.*

I slip out the back door, stockinged feet soaking up dew from the damp grass. The air flickers around the honeysuckle as I approach. I hear his voice, floating from behind the fence, calling to me. I stop at the crux of the crisscrossing branches, drooping heavily with blooms. There, in front of the gate, was a perfect fairy circle of dog figurines. My baby is here. Just beyond the toys, a dark recess widens up between the branches. The honeysuckle gate opens and Rudy's voice floats through, my heart twisting in recognition.

"See Go? Hi, hi, Maum-Maum-Maum. Om ear, Maum."

I hesitate, feeling the pulsating pain that still radiates from the wound on my hip. Since that night, a new Rudy appeared, looking to all the world like my baby boy, but nevertheless, not my baby boy at all. I turn, looking back at the house into his bedroom window. He isn't there, not anymore. I step into the circle and cross the gate.

"Rudy, baby. It's mommy," I call.

"Hi, Maum-Maum."

I pull back the plaster and step through the wall.

Emily Fox-Douglas

Emily **Fox-Douglas** is a writer of horror, magical realism, and poetry. Her work has been featured in Haunted Waters Press and *Parhelion Literary Magazine*. When she is not writing, you can find her camping with her family and stargazing into the abyss. Emily lives in Ohio with her husband and two children.

Bibliography

If Time Were a Shutter Click, Haunted Waters Press, 2019
"Spiderwalk," *Parhelion Literary Magazine*, 2021

Connect

Twitter: @emilyfoxinsocks
Facebook: facebook.com/emily.fox.7587
Instagram: @emily_foxinsocks

Macabre Minima

Macabre Minima is a small, independent publisher based in Melbourne, Australia. Founded in 2018, our aim has always been to champion emerging authors from all around the globe and offer opportunities for them to participate in speculative fiction and horror short story anthologies.

Emily Fox-Douglas

Coming Soon

What Blood is For

by Nyx Kain

He snugged the blanket up under her chin. His fingers held the linen line of it there a moment longer, taut as her arms tucked to her sides and her legs together at the ankles.

The light from the open door broke across his back and caught rapt shards in his eyes. Who was he looking at?

The question beat in the held space of Abigail's breath. It seemed to wait for her every night now, right where the impression of her body in the mattress placed her heart. But she pinned it in place with her weight, and he was the one to speak.

"Is something wrong, child?"

She unstuck her tongue from the roof of her mouth. Tried to let out that beating breath without letting him hear how long it had been aching in her lungs.

"Nothing," she said with just the last of it. "I was thinking of Mother."

The light told her so little about how he was looking at

her. Shards and the stoop of his shoulders. Stillness in the long seconds before he answered.

"Is that so?"

She nodded against the pillow. Tucked her swallow under the blanket. "I was thinking of what happened," she said. "It doesn't seem fair. You said last week that God is always just. How was it just to let her die like that?"

Her heart hammered and her fingers twisted tight into her nightgown. The question throbbed like a hot, glowing bruise, something he should have been able to see through her, shining.

Maybe he could. Whoever he saw when he looked at her, he didn't seem to like them. Not standing there, not lately.

"God's justice doesn't always look like ours," he said. Stepping back from the bed, just enough so she could see the flex of skin across hollow cheeks as he spoke. "It could be He intended to keep her from some suffering that would have fouled her spirit. Or to prevent her from compromising the spiritual walks of others."

"She would never have." She hadn't meant to speak. It seemed dangerous lying there, lately, to do so without checking her words for the question first. "She never hurt anyone."

"Not intentionally, I'm sure. Try not to trouble yourself too much with this," he urged her. "It isn't always ours to understand. Sometimes, the best we can do is to walk in gratitude, and trust that our immortal interests are being seen to. Sleep well."

Two words as solid and warning as *the end*. Wherever the story might go past that point, the listener was forbidden to follow. She nodded again, crushing a hard clump of words under her chin, against her chest.

He watched a few seconds longer, as if to be sure she had swallowed them. Then turned away, his face to light as it left her sight. The fists drawn tight at his sides to shadow.

His shadow lingered by her bedside, long and bent, until he shut the door behind him. The dark settled gray over her face then, the folds in the blanket where her fists had caught it tight. The breath she let out long and trembling, at last, into a silence that wouldn't ask her why she seemed so afraid.

* 9 7 9 8 2 2 3 2 1 9 5 0 7 *